Jay Bird

Jay Bird

Written and illustrated by
MARIE HALL ETS

The Viking Press   *New York*

1 2 3 4 5 78 77 76 75 74

Library of Congress Cataloging in Publication Data

Ets, Marie Hall, 1895–   Jay bird.

Summary: During one day a little boy hears such
sounds as a jay bird scolding, oak leaves swaying,
and a mother humming.   [1. Sounds—Fiction]

I. Title.   PZ7.E855Jay   [E]   73-19590

ISBN 0-670-40608-2

Also by Marie Hall Ets

Elephant in a Well

Talking Without Words

Beasts and Nonsense

Just Me

Automobiles for Mice

Gilberto and the Wind

Play with Me

Another Day

Mr. T. W. Anthony Woo

Little Old Automobile

Oley: The Sea Monster

In the Forest

The Story of a Baby

Nine Days to Christmas
(with Aurora Labastida)

My Dog Rinty
(with Ellen Tarry)

Jay Bird

A JAY BIRD scolding
   in a tree.
Scolding, scolding, scolding.

A HOPTOAD croaking
in the swamp.
Croaking, croaking, croaking.

A BILLY GOAT baaing
in the field.
Baaing, baaing, baaing.

A TOMCAT yowling
   in the alley.
Yowling, yowling, yowling.

A LITTLE BOY slowly walking
to school.
Walking, walking, walking.

OAK LEAVES swaying
in the wind.
Swaying, swaying, swaying.

An AIRPLANE buzzing
across the sky.
Buzzing, buzzing, buzzing.

A MOO COW tinkling
    her bell.
Tinkling, tinkling, tinkling.

A MOTHER humming
   to her child.
Humming, humming, humming.

A ROOSTER crowing
    at the sun.
Crowing, crowing, crowing.

A HOUND-DOG barking
at the moon.
Barking, barking, barking.

A LITTLE BOY talking
to a toad.
Talking, talking, talking.

Goodnight, JAY BIRD,
scolding in the tree.

Goodnight, HOPTOAD,
croaking in the swamp.

Goodnight, LITTLE BOY,
getting ready for bed.

Goodnight, EVERYBODY.

GOODNIGHT.

Goodnight.